GW00836397

The Three
Little Pigs

This book belongs to

Aimee

This much-loved fairytale is humorously retold and illustrated by the best-selling children's author and artist, Richard Scarry. He has written and illustrated more than 300 books, published worldwide in over 30 different languages.

This fairytale is ideally suited to be read to children or for beginner readers to enjoy reading for themselves.

Richard Scarry

The Three Little Pigs

Published in Great Britain in 1993 with the authorization
of Les Livres du Dragon d'Or by
World International Publishing Limited,
an Egmont Company, Egmont House, PO Box 111,
Great Ducie Street, Manchester M60 3BL.

Printed in Germany.   ISBN 0 7498 1399 7

A catalogue record for this book is available from the British Library.

Once upon a time there were three little pigs. When they were old enough they left home to seek their fortunes.

Mother Pig was very sad
to see them leave.

The first little pig met a farmer with a load of straw.

"Please sir," he said, "will you give me some straw to build a house?"

The farmer gave the first little pig some straw.

The little pig used the straw to build a house.

Along came a wicked wolf and knocked on the door.

"Little pig, little pig, let me come in," said the wolf.

But the little pig answered, "No, no! Not by the hair of my chinny chin chin."

"Then I'll huff and I'll puff and I'll blow your house in," said the wolf.

And he huffed and he puffed
and he blew the house in,
and he ate the little pig up.

The second little pig met a woodcutter
with a bundle of sticks.

"Please sir," he asked, "may I have some
sticks to build a house?"

The woodcutter gave him some sticks
and the second little pig built his house of
sticks.

Then along came the wolf, who said,
"Little pig, little pig, let me come in."

"No, no! Not by the hair of my chinny chin chin," answered the second little pig.

"Then I'll huff and I'll puff and I'll blow your house in," said the wolf.

And he huffed and he puffed,
and he huffed and he puffed,
and he blew the house in,
and ate the second little pig up.

The third little pig met a bricklayer
with a load of bricks.

"Please sir," he asked, "may I have some
bricks to build a house?"

The bricklayer gave him some bricks and
the third little pig built his house of bricks.

Then along came
the wolf, who said,
"Little pig, little pig,
let me come in."

And the third little pig answered,
"No, no! Not by the hair of my chinny chin
chin."

"Then I'll huff and I'll puff and I'll blow
your house in," said the wolf.

So the wolf huffed and he puffed,
and he huffed and he puffed.

He huffed and
he puffed until
he could huff
and puff no more.

But he could not
blow the little house in.

"I must think of a trick to get that little
pig out of his house," the crafty wolf said
to himself.

After thinking for a while he said,
"Little pig, I know of a garden where
there are some tasty turnips. Will you join
me at seven o'clock tomorrow morning
and we will go and get some?"

"Where are they?" asked the little pig.
"Down in Green Fields," said the wolf.
The little pig agreed to go.

When the wolf came at seven o'clock the next day he asked the little pig if he was ready to go.

"Why, I have been there already," said the little pig, "and have brought home a basketful of turnips for dinner."

The wolf was very angry at this, but he pretended not to be.

The following day the wolf
came to the little pig's house again.

"Little pig, there is a fair at Good Town
this afternoon. Will you go with me?" he
asked.

"Oh, yes," said the little pig. "When
shall I meet you?"

"At three o'clock," said the wolf.

So the little pig, as before, went earlier.
At the fair he bought a butter churn to
make butter in.

As he was going home with it he saw the
wolf coming up the road. He didn't know
what to do.

He decided to
climb into the
churn to hide.

But the churn tipped over and rolled
down the hill.

The wolf was so frightened by it that he
ran away home without going to the fair
to find the little pig.

Now when the wolf found out that the
little pig had been inside the churn,
he was furious.

He went to the little pig's house.

"Little pig, little pig," he called, "you got away from me at Green Fields and the Good Town fair, but you can't get away from me now.

I am coming down the chimney to eat you up!"

Well, the little pig quickly took the lid
off the big pot of soup on the fire . . .

SPLASH! Into the hot soup fell the wolf!

The wolf jumped up and ran howling out of the door, never to return to the little brick house where the little pig lived happily ever after. Wasn't the little pig clever to outwit the wolf?